The Greatest Church in the World

This is the story of every pastor.

At some point, nearly every pastor questions whether he or she has made the right decision to go into the ministry.

It is the story of every church.

Every church has the potential to get off track and lose focus. Every church is challenged with worldly distractions.

It is a story for every congregation.

There is hope for every church to become The Greatest Church in the World. The principles taught in this story are universal truths that can guide a church and keep it focused on what matters most.

Praise for The Greatest Church in the World

A must read

This book is a blessing and a "must read" for two special groups of people: those who are discouraged with what they have experienced with "church" and are thinking of leaving, and those who love their local church but sense that there must be more to the Christian life than what they have experienced. *The Greatest Church in the World* describes the church that I have sought for more than 45 years, but have only tasted for seasons that are always too short. Read the book. You will be encouraged.

Buck Jacobs
Author and Founder of C12 Group

Every church has the potential

Every church has the potential. The question is, "Do I want my church to be *that* church? Do I will that my church be so and am I willing to pay the price?"

Skip Carney gives the game plan in an outstanding presentation. It's a quick read with clear direction shared in a parable type format.

I urge you to read and share this book.

Dois Rosser
Founder of International Cooperating Ministries

It is time for change

The church in America must be transformed! A majority are stagnant or shrinking. This book outlines the path to the church Jesus commanded us to take. Since 2006, we have coached thousands of pastors these principles with enormous spiritual fruit as a result. Now, we will use this book as our guide to mentor and coach pastors, church leaders and church members. This is the new handbook for a transformed church.

A must read followed by much prayer!

Martin Newby
Founder of LoveServes.org

For every church member AND everyone else

The Greatest Church in the World portrays the church that nearly everyone can embrace. It is a church without pretense or fences. It is a church that simplifies discipleship and encourages participation. This is the church that can re-energize Christianity in America – indeed the world.

Chuck Verrett
Founder of Sustainable Mission Partners

This book is for the church today!

It will not be needed 25 years from now as the only churches that will remain will be doing these things.

Richard Reising
Author of *Church Marketing 101*

Inspirational

The Greatest Church in the World gives me hope. Hope that churches will focus on what matters most. That they will actively reach out to their communities and make a difference. And it gives me hope that the unreached will come to know and embrace Jesus in a way that profoundly impacts their lives for good.

Dr. Dewey Clark
Past President of NC Wesleyan College

What millennials are searching for

This is a story that needs to be told, studied, understood and lived. When these beacons are adopted and internalized, churches thrive, are vibrant, and alive. When they are ignored, churches find themselves lost, stagnant, and struggling.

These beacons will attract millennials and GenXers while retaining baby boomers. Most importantly, they will allow the unchurched the opportunity to explore God's word and witness God's grace.

Executive Pastor (retired) Rick Carney
Mooresville, NC

This book will change lives

As a minister for more than 30 years, I have seen too many churches struggle because they failed to embrace the principles in this book. I have also seen churches find new purpose and excitement whenever they followed these beacons.

Rev. John Check
Rocky Mount, NC

A fun and stimulating book.

This book strips all of the stupidity and mindlessness out of dying church stuff. And brings it back to life again. It brings us to timeless principles that churches, all churches, need all of to live.

There are a number of "10 principles" books out there. Many of them focus on what an alive church *does*. What I like about this one is, it focuses on the ten things an alive church *is*.

Pastor Jeff Arnold
Beaver, PA

The Greatest Church in the World

The Greatest Church in the World

A Lamp on a Hill

by Skip Carney

Requests for information should be addressed to:
The Foundation for Christian Education, P.O. Box 7398, Rocky Mount, NC 27804 or info@skipcarney.com.

Dedication

This book is dedicated to my wife, Karen, and daughters Jessica, Kathryn, and Spencer Grace. To my mother, who taught me to believe that anything is possible. And my dad, who always encouraged me to make myself useful.

Acknowledgments

In 1979, I was about to start a business. I had almost zero business experience, no money, a mortgage, and a growing family. My dad, a very practical kind of guy, surprised me with words of encouragement and a book. The book was written by a man with a strange name – Og Mandino. That book, *The Greatest Salesman in the World*, has been on my desk ever since. The cover is gone. The pages are tattered and brown with age, but the words still inspire and guide me to this day. Og's style of writing and his simple method of communicating powerful concepts has influenced me in countless ways, not the least of which is this book. Og has left this world, but his words will live forever, and I am thankful.

I have also found inspiration from Rick Warren's Daily Hope and the writings of Thom Rainer, Francis Chan, and Mark Batterson. These men are doing great work for the body of Christ. I continue to learn and grow from their teaching, example, and courage.

In 2012, I joined a peer advisory group called C12. That decision was pivotal in my journey. Thanks to C12, I am knee-deep in the Bible and eager to go deeper. Without C12, I would only be "scan" deep. I thank Robert Beaman, Steve Calhoun, and founder Buck Jacobs for their patience and encouragement.

When I was struggling to find my voice for this project, my brother Rick – the strongest, gentlest Christian I know – sent me a simple text that totally changed my perspective and thinking. He suggested that I focus on helping the "people" rather than the "church." This book is the direct result of that message.

Lastly, I thank my wife, Karen. She has, quite amazingly, followed and quietly guided me on my journey. She has given me the space and time to figure things out on my own and she has magically stepped in with answers to questions that I didn't even realize I was asking. Her quiet strength, unconditional love, and confidence have given me the support and freedom I needed and continue to need.

Introduction

I used to believe that we are the sum total of our experiences, education, and knowledge combined with our personality, drive, and talents. I was wrong. Now, I know that when we combine those ingredients with God's purpose and power, we are exponentially more than we could ever imagine or could ever be otherwise. Humans add. God multiplies.

I believe this is also true of the Church. Every church, no matter how large or small, rich or poor can be The Greatest Church in the World when it works in concert with our Maker.

This story and the principles in this book came from observation, study, meditation, and prayer. My prayer for you is that you find inspiration, clarification, and freedom in the words of this book. Freedom to focus on the things that matter most. Freedom to make a dramatic difference in your community. Freedom to see a better future for your church and thus, the body of Christ.

My hope is that you will see a path to help your church become The Greatest Church in the World.

Skip Carney

The Foundation for Christian Education

All proceeds from the sale of this book go directly to the Foundation for Christian Education, a 501(c)(3) not-for-profit organization. The purpose of the foundation is to develop, promote, and implement Christian educational content and materials for students of all ages.

To order bulk quantities of this book, study guides, Beacon Booklets, Be the Light window decals, and to join our email list, visit:

www.foundationforchristianeducation.com

A Lamp on a Hill

In the same way, let your light shine before others, that they may see your good deeds and glorify your Father in heaven.

Matthew 5:16

This is the message we have heard from Him and declare to you: God is light; in Him there is no darkness at all. But if we walk in the light, as He is in the light, we have fellowship with one another, and the blood of Jesus, His Son, purifies us from all sin.

1 John 1:5, 7

Saturday

It was black-and-white time. That time just after dusk, but before dark, when all the color is gone from the landscape. Everything was black and white and Kevin was three hundred and forty-seven miles from home. It was a Saturday evening in December, and he had just pulled off the interstate. He sat at the end of the exit ramp as he watched the lights change. He was deep in thought. The lights flashed, they changed, he watched. He was still thinking. Not moving. There was no traffic. So what did it matter? That was the question, wasn't it? What really matters? "What really matters?" He said it out loud. "I guess I really am lost."

Kevin needed to make a decision. He decided to turn to the right. He eased onto the two-lane blacktop. There were faint signs of life in that direction. There was smoke rising from a chimney about a quarter of a mile away. As he passed, he saw Christmas lights shining through the window. *I need to call Grace,* he thought. *But not yet.*

Not yet. He passed a small billboard with the image of a lighthouse and the words **PEACE Awaits Within**. *I could use some of that,* he thought.

He drove into town, turning onto Main Street. The last of the sunlight was gone now and the street lights flickered on. The street was quiet, and he felt like he had driven back in time. "A real hardware store," he mused. He passed the funeral home, a men's clothing store, and the pharmacy – all dark. "I guess they roll up the sidewalks on Saturday nights around here," he chuckled.

He parked the car on the street and got out to stretch his legs. A cold wind caught him by surprise as the last remnants of fall cascaded in his direction from a nearby oak tree. *Winter is close,* he thought. He glanced at his reflection in the department store window. The touches of gray that added the salt to his pepper-black hair, the faint lines around his eyes. He was getting used to those signs of age – "signs of maturity," according to Grace. He couldn't get used to what was missing, though. The spark in his eyes, the spring in his step. The feeling of anticipation that each day was going to be better than the last. The feeling that he was here for a purpose, a great purpose. Now, he was overcome with a sense of failure. He had let himself down. He felt like he had let his family down. And God. He had let God down.

As he walked through the silent town, he could hear the sound of his footsteps echoing off the buildings across the street. Empty and alone. The sound seemed to remind him that he would not be preaching tomorrow morning. No committee meetings next week. No programs to plan.

His calendar was empty, and he felt empty, too. He had told Grace he was going to take a couple of days to think and pray and decide what was next. He started driving that morning. When the big 'E' appeared on his dashboard, he decided it was time to pull over, *here in the middle of nowhere*, he thought. *I don't even know the name of this town.*

He looked up. There was light at the end of the street, and it grew as he approached. *Maybe a diner*, he thought. *I could use a cup of coffee and a smile.* It wasn't a diner. It was a small lighthouse in front of a small church. *Ironic*, he thought. *At least I can get warm – if the doors are open.*

He tugged at the brass knob on the heavy wooden door. He saw light beaming through the leaded glass portal and he could see the sanctuary was empty. The door swung open. He could feel the warmth as he stepped inside. He shook off the chill, slipped off his coat, and walked down the carpet-covered aisle past the well-worn wooden pews. The red hymnals and the black prayer books were just like in the church where he grew up. It was very, very quiet. He took a seat and opened his Bible. He shivered, but not from the cold. It was time to decide.

He started. "God, I'm sorry. I … uh … don't know what to do. Maybe I'm just not right for this job." He paused and took a deep breath. He was just about to say "I quit" when he realized he was not alone. He looked up and into the face of a gentleman coming down the aisle. He knew at once this man was the pastor of this little church.

"What job?" said the elder pastor.

Kevin caught his breath. He coughed. He looked deeply into the face of this man he had never seen before – a face that was both friendly and comfortable. The wrinkles around his eyes reflected years of smiles … and peace. That was it. Kevin felt peace radiate from this old stranger.

"If I had to guess, I'd say you're a pastor, aren't you?" the old man offered.

"How did you know … ?" Kevin trailed off.

"I've been expecting you. I'm Pastor Tom. You can call me Tom," he said. The calm in his voice, the gleam in his eyes were beyond reassuring. Kevin felt like he had known him a long time.

"I'm Kevin. But Tom, how did you know?"

"You sounded like you were talking to your boss about your job," he chuckled. "If God is your boss, you must be a pastor."

"What do you mean you were expecting me?" Kevin asked.

"Something told me to hang around a little longer tonight, so I did," he said. "Sounds like you've been through a pretty tough season."

Kevin grunted.

"Sounded like you were about to quit."

"I am – or I was," he said.

"I know the feeling," Tom offered.

"How's that?" Kevin asked. "Seems like you have a nice little church here. You look … uh, happy … content," he added.

"I am. I take it you are not. How long?"

"I graduated from seminary six and a half years ago," Kevin said. "My first call was ideal, at least I thought it would be. The pastor was retiring after 32 years of service. We hit it off immediately. It was the same with the search committee. It seemed like the perfect fit. The church was still strong but had seen decline in attendance and membership. The committee wanted new ideas, growth, and a fresh perspective. It was perfect."

"And?" Tom took a seat beside Kevin.

"It was a perfect disaster," he said, shaking his head. "After three and a half years of no change and continued decline, I took a position at a contemporary church with a more 'progressive' leadership team."

"You added the air quotes around 'progressive' because?"

"We progressed from one program to another for no apparent reason and, in all the busy-ness of the days and weeks and months, we spent less and less time praying and more and more time playing. That's one of the reasons I apologized to God."

"So now you are ready to quit?" asked Tom with a strange smile on his face.

Kevin answered without saying a word.

"You look beat. I take it you're a long way from home," Tom offered as he stood. "There's a diner just down the street and the motel next door has a warm room for you, my treat."

"I uh … "

"I insist. The owner is a member of our church. He's always taking in strays," Tom chuckled.

"I … "

"I insist." Pastor Tom paused. "And I insist you return tomorrow morning for our 10:30 service."

Kevin stood and started to put on his coat.
"Our church was once like yours," added Pastor Tom.

"Which one?"

"Both." Tom smiled. "I'll see you in the morning. Things are always better in the morning."

Kevin finished his meal. Meatloaf, homemade pie, a cup of coffee, and a smile from a girl named Abby. Kevin was still deep in thought. He had called Grace earlier. As always, she had been understanding and supportive when he called. She was glad he had found a place to stop. "It sounds like a nice town," she said. "Maybe Pastor Tom and the Lighthouse church are just what you need."

He shook his head. *This town, this church, are nothing like my towns or churches. Well, maybe I'll hear a good sermon,* he thought. *Me and the twenty-five members of the Lighthouse.* He paid his bill and headed to the motel. There was a small sticker on the door of the motel office. It read **Rest Here**. In the lower right hand corner was the image of a small lighthouse.

Sunday

Snow fell during the night. Only a few inches, but it transformed the town. The dark, empty streets were now bright and cheery. As he drove away from the motel, Kevin sensed things were better today. He noticed the Christmas decorations on the lamp posts and in the store windows.

As he turned onto Main Street, he came to a complete stop. He couldn't believe his eyes. Downtown was bustling. Every parking spot was taken. The sidewalks were filled with families – moms, dads, and children. And they were all headed toward the lighthouse at the end of the street. A car honked behind him. *Wow,* he thought. *Guess I better find a place to park.*

He left his car in the bank lot and started walking toward the church. He could hear the music from a block away, and on the front lawn of the church, someone was pouring hot chocolate and coffee. Folks were talking on the lawn, oblivious to the cold and the snow. Others were heading inside to warm up and get a seat. *It's only 9:45. I thought I was getting here early,* Kevin thought as he stared at his watch. *Maybe it's a special service.*

It was not a special service, but the service was special. Kevin had never seen the kind of enthusiasm he witnessed today. He had never felt the Spirit as strong as today. Everyone was engaged. Everyone was involved. Everyone was … comfortable. That was it. They were comfortable. The visitors, the children, everyone seemed to belong. Kevin felt comfortable, but it made him uncomfortable that he didn't know why or how he could feel that way on his first visit to a strange church in a strange town. A strange town that didn't feel strange.

After church, Kevin waited for his chance to speak with Pastor Tom. He watched as people lingered to talk. There were hugs and laughter. There were couples drinking coffee and tea. No one was in a hurry to leave. "This is odd," Kevin said under his breath. As he approached, Pastor Tom took a seat on the steps near the altar.

"What was that?" Kevin queried. "How … ?" He was at a loss for words.

"Take a seat," Tom offered.

"You said your church was just like mine," he blurted.

"It used to be, Kevin. Just a few years ago, this church was just like your churches."

"Pastor. We had attendance. We had praise and worship. We had members," Kevin paused. "What I saw here was participation, engagement. I saw love. I saw something today that I have never seen before. How … ?"

"We used to be like yours and many other churches. People without purpose. Membership without mission.

We had some very strong members who were very committed," Tom said, shaking his head.

"Committed to what?" asked Kevin.

"That was the problem, Kevin. We forgot why we were here. Like many congregations, we lost focus. We were just – lost." The Pastor lingered. "Just a few years ago, we had dwindled to thirty-three families and Sunday morning attendance rarely topped twenty."

"What happened?"

Pastor Tom laughed. "We prayed."

Kevin waited for the rest.

"That's it, Kevin. We prayed as a church. Every member. Every day. Until we started to see the light. Slowly, over time, we discovered the ten principles that guide us today."

"Ten principles? Like the Ten Commandments?" asked Kevin.

"Well, we call them Beacons – they illuminate our path. Guide us when we are not sure which way to turn. Get us through stormy weather."

"Like a lighthouse?" mused Kevin.

"Like a lighthouse," said Tom. "Not very original, I admit."

Kevin fidgeted in his seat. The sanctuary was empty now. Kevin could feel his heartbeat.

"Pastor. Tom."

"Yes?"

"Pastor. Is this real? Is this a normal Sunday for The Lighthouse Church?"

"It is."

"I've never seen anything like it." He paused. "I want this. I mean, I want to learn how you did this. How you do this. You just might have the greatest church in the world here."

"We think we do, Kevin."

"What I mean is: can this be done at other churches?"

"Sure it can."

"Can you teach me?"

"Can you stay a while?"

"I can stay as long as it takes."

"Give me a week," Tom smiled. "Meet me here tomorrow morning at nine."

Monday

"Here's your change, Pastor. How was your breakfast?"

"Thanks, Abby. Just right. It hit the spot."

The waitress smiled. "I hear you're going to be here for a few days."

"News travels fast in this town, doesn't it?" Kevin left a tip and headed out the door. "See you tomorrow," he said over his shoulder.

He had decided to walk the half mile to the church. The morning air was brisk but the sun was warm on his face. "The greatest church in the world," he said out loud. "Did I really say that? Maybe I am going crazy."

"Crazy about what?"

Kevin looked in the direction of the question. It was Abby. She was holding the hat he had left in the diner.

"Oh, I was just thinking about what I saw at the church yesterday."

"The Lighthouse. Isn't it great?" She added.

11

"It sure seems like it to me," Kevin said, taking his hat. "But can a church be that good every week? Is that really possible?"

"It is here. Ever since this." She pulled a small book out of her pocket. Kevin had seen that book the day before. Many in the congregation carried it with their Bibles.

"The Beacons?"

"You should have a copy."

"I hope to get one today," he said.

"Awesome. You'll see. It is the greatest church in the world." Abby smiled as she turned and skipped back to the diner.

Kevin put his hat on and continued toward the Lighthouse. The snowman in the front yard of the church had a handwritten, cardboard sign that read Welcome. Hope is Here. He entered through the side door, looking for the church office. Inside, he passed a small group sorting groceries into cardboard boxes.

"What's this?" he said to no one in particular.

"Our food bank. This is what we collected yesterday."

"For Lighthouse members?"

"Yes, sir. Or anyone in the community who needs food."

Kevin continued through the short, paneled hallway. He found Pastor Tom in the sanctuary. He was reading. He looked up when he heard Kevin approach.

"Good morning, Pastor. Take a seat."

"Is there always this much activity here at the Lighthouse?"

"Of course."

Kevin was about to ask another question when the front door to the sanctuary swung open. The glare from the sunlight outside followed the silhouette of a lady into the great hall. Kevin couldn't see her face, but he sensed this was a woman of confidence, poise. As she approached, he could see she was dressed for business. Not "corporate" exactly, but definitely business.

"And here's our Mayor," exclaimed Tom. "Janet, this is Kevin. The Pastor I told you about. He has questions."

"That's an understatement," said Kevin as he stood. "Glad to meet you, ma'am – uh – mayor."

"Janet, please. There's no protocol here at the Lighthouse."

"Janet is a member here, Kevin. She will answer some of your questions. I'll check back with you later," said Tom, slipping toward the door.

"But, Pastor … "

"You're in good hands, son. Janet will teach you."

He watched as Tom disappeared down the hallway. He turned to Janet. "What does he mean? You will teach me."

"You want to know how did this little church become what you saw yesterday, such a vital part of this community, correct?"

"Is it really? A vital part of the community?"

"Absolutely," she answered. "Not just the town. This little lighthouse has made a difference with the church community in the entire area, and the businesses, and the charities, and … "

"How?" Kevin queried.

"I'm sure Pastor Tom told you it all began when we were, literally, about to close our doors. We came together and prayed."

"He did. He said you 'saw the light'."

"We did. Once we dropped everything else and focused on what God wanted for us, it was like the scales fell from our eyes."

"So, what was the first 'revelation'?"

"It wasn't a revelation, Kevin. It was prayer."

"I know, but ... "

"That was it, Kevin. The first step was just that simple. We put our trust in God."

Kevin turned his head sideways, the way a puppy does when it is trying to understand its master. She handed him a small book. It was the same book Pastor Tom was reading, and it was the book Abby had pulled out of her pocket. It had an elegant but simple cover with the emblem of the lighthouse embossed into the leather. It was well-worn, the pages dog-eared and bookmarked. He saw highlights and writing in the margins as he thumbed through the pages.

"What is this?" he asked.

"That's my copy of The Lighthouse Beacons. Here is yours," she said as she handed him a new copy of the book. "Read the first chapter. I'll be back in a bit."

"But ... " She was gone. Kevin settled back in the pew and opened the little book. "It can't be this simple," he said to himself.

Trust in the Lord with all your heart and lean not on your own understanding: in all your ways submit to Him and He will make your paths straight.

Proverbs 3:5-6

Those who know your name trust in you, for you, Lord, have never forsaken those who seek you.

Psalm 9:10

Now all glory to God, who is able, through His mighty power at work within us, to accomplish infinitely more than we might ask or think.

Ephesians 3:20 (NLT)

Beacon Number One

We will trust God.

We know our church has a purpose. We know we have lost our way. We thought it was our job to run the church; that every decision was ours to make. We thought we could keep God in the back seat while we drove. We were wrong. Today, we are crumbling beneath the weight of such foolishness.

Today, we will trust God.

We have spent too much time seeking the wrong things. Our focus has been scattered, our vision unclear. We have fought *with* each other instead of *for* each other. We have built silos that isolated us and walls that separated us. King David said, "Joyful are people of integrity, who follow the instructions of the Lord" (Psalm 119:1 NLT). We have not been joyful. We have not followed the Lord's instructions.

We will trust God.

And how will we trust God? With all our hearts, our minds, and our souls. We will pray. We will pray together. We will seek His Word, His guidance, His glory. We will follow His direction and take our seat in the back while He drives. We know that without God, we will surely fail. Our job is bigger than us, bigger than any person or any church. We can only succeed with God's help.

Today, we will trust God.

We will trust God with patience and faithfulness. With expectation and joy. We know everything happens in God's time and not ours. It is our job to plant the seeds, to till the soil, and reap the harvest. We will work patiently until the harvest is ready. We will never put off until tomorrow the work that must be done today. We may toil with little result, but we know if we are working for God, we are working for Good.

We know our job. We are to reach the unreached. To share the Good News. To guide the faithful. To love God. How we do that is different for every church, for every community. We will use these beacons as guides to follow God's path for this church and this community.

We will trust God.

Our church is young though it is decades old. It is still a child learning to walk, a bird learning to fly. Though we are young, our foundation is centuries old and it contains principles that will endure forever. Principles written in stone by God's own hand. Yesterday, we suffered because we forgot those principles – those beacons of light. Our God defined our purpose long before our building was built and long before the first sermon was preached or the first person was baptized. Today, we follow those principles. We will pray. We will listen.

We will trust God.

Kevin looked up from the book. Janet was back. "My churches … we prayed. We trusted God. I think we did … "

"Yes, we thought we did, too." Janet sat down beside him. "But there is a difference between asking for God to accomplish your goals and getting on your knees to ask His goals," she said. "We got down on our knees, Kevin. From that perspective, we saw that we were missing the point. We spent too much time and energy looking inwardly. The people that needed us most were outside the church and we rarely reached out to them. We rarely invited them in. We were too busy. We thought we were doing good things, Kevin. We had good intentions."

"So you got back to basics," Kevin said. He was looking into the book, absorbing the words on the pages and the words between the lines. "You started over, didn't you?"

"That's right," said Janet. "God starts every day new and fresh. We decided we could, too. I have a meeting in a few minutes," she said. "Turn the page, Kevin. Beacon Number Two is all about starting fresh."

Janet stepped out of the pew and into the shadows.

A Lamp on a Hill

Sometimes people say, "Here is something new!" But actually it's old. Nothing is ever truly new.

Ecclesiastes 1:10 (NLT)

Beacon Number Two

Today, our church is new.

Yesterday, we were old. We were tired. We were fighting. We were clinging to the past. Today, our church is new. Yesterday, we focused on very little. We were busy picking nits and building silos. We didn't see what we couldn't see because our eyes were focused on the wrong things.

Today, our church is new.

Yesterday, we lived in the past. We measured every decision by what used to be, or what used to work, or what didn't work. Yesterday, we were led by men and women. Today, we trust in God. We recognize that the past has passed. Our successes and failures of the past hold us back. They paralyze our thinking and hamper our actions. They cause us to second guess ourselves and each other.

Today, our church is new.

How will we act, now that we are new? Today, we embrace the present and await the future with confidence. We ignore the actions of others. We ignore the fads of the day and the whims of those who would have us try something "just because it is new." Today, we ignore those shiny distractions. We will welcome change, not for change's sake but because the world is changing. Today, the world moves faster. Communication is instantaneous. Information is everywhere. If we fail to embrace the present, we will leave a void where the Word should be. We will not give the advantage to the evil one. We will change — not in defense, but in offense. We have the greatest message in the world for the people of the world. We will change so we can share that message.

Today, our church is new.

Every day is a new day. We will treat each day as such. We will open our eyes to see the beauty of each day. We will open our ears to hear the voices of the present. We will open our hearts to the needs of others. We will open our doors to our community. We will welcome new faces, new ideas, new thinking. New people will bring us new life, new energy and new opportunities to serve. Isn't that why we are here? To serve?

Today, our church is new.

Our charge is old. We are to make disciples —
to spread the Good News. We are to love God
and one another. These directives will never
change. They will never grow old. But our church
must change to fulfill our purpose. Our charge is
old, but our church is new. Whenever we start to
get comfortable or proud or content, we will remember our charge and we will look for new
ways to make our church new and relevant and
purposeful. We will welcome the questions that
start with "why." Why do we do it this way? Why
don't we try something different? Whenever the
answer is "We've always done it that way," we
will remember this beacon. We will look for new
answers, new solutions, and we will thank those
who challenged the old, tired ways. We will con-
stantly look for ways to keep things fresh, different
and new, but always focused on our purpose – to
share the Good News and love our neighbor.

Today, our church is new.

Kevin closed his eyes, allowing the words to sink in.

"What do you think?" Janet had slipped in through
the side door.

"Pretty gutsy, starting over," he said. "I guess it was
easier with such a small group."

"Anything but," she replied. "Some of our strongest members fought the whole idea. I was one of them."

"So, how did you … ? "

"God won," she said. "In the end – or the new beginning – it was clear we were not getting our job done. We were failing."

"Because you were shrinking? Because you weren't growing?"

"Because there were people in this community who needed God, Kevin, and we were too 'busy' to help them find Him. We were so committed to the past that we were blind to the present and the future."

"You forgot your purpose," Kevin mused, half under his breath.

"We forgot our purpose. So when we turned to God and prayed, it became clear we had to wipe away the old thinking and start fresh."

"So, what happened next? How did you do it?"

"It wasn't easy," she said. "But God was with us."

The morning flew by as Janet answered Kevin's questions. They talked about The Lighthouse and they talked about his experience of the past six years. By noon, Kevin was excited and exhausted. His mind was working overtime to absorb the meaning of Beacons One and Two.

"Kevin, I think this is enough for today. Take the rest of the day to reflect on what you've learned. Read and re-read these Beacons. Tomorrow, you'll meet Michael, one of the younger leaders in The Lighthouse." With that, Janet said goodbye.

Kevin was alone. For the first time in years, he didn't feel alone.

He called Grace as he walked back toward the motel. "I've learned so much already. I'm starting to see what went wrong these past years," he said, struggling to contain his excitement. "I'm sorry I'm so far from home."

"It's okay," she assured him. "You are starting to sound like the man I married. Bring that man back and all is good." She laughed.

Kevin chuckled and glanced at his reflection in the hardware store window. *How 'bout that – a smile.* He spent the rest of the day contemplating the meaning and application of Beacons One and Two. And he prayed.

The Greatest Church in the World

Tuesday

Kevin was up early the next day. He was eager to learn more. He was about to walk out the door when he heard a knock. He glanced at his watch. *7:05? Hmmmm.* He opened the door. It was Janet.

"Good morning, Mayor – I mean, Janet."

"We thought you would be up." She reached to shake his hand. "Kevin, I want you to meet Michael."

Kevin hadn't noticed the young man standing beside her.

"Hi, Kevin," he said.

"Oh, hi Michael." At first glance, he thought maybe Michael was a college student. Then again, everyone under twenty-five looked "young" now.

He was about to ask a question when Janet intervened, "Let's go grab a cup of coffee."

They settled into their seats in the coffee shop, an eclectic little place with comfy sofas, handmade tables, and local artwork on the walls. Kevin noticed a small decal on the wall: **Kindness Starts Here**. It had a lighthouse image in the lower right corner.

"Michael is active at The Lighthouse. He and his wife have helped us a lot."

"You're married?" Kevin asked.

"Sure. Three years now."

Kevin was letting that sink in. It was nearly impossible to get young couples involved in his churches. They were just too busy or uninterested.

"Michael, how did you get involved? Did you grow up in this church?"

"We moved here a couple of years ago. Before our daughter was born."

"So, you were looking for a church?"

"Not really. We were kind of ambivalent about 'religion'."

"So, how ... ?"

"One Saturday my neighbor invited me to have coffee." Michael grinned. "It was a group of sixteen other men. They talked about issues in the community and issues within the church. That's when I met Pastor Tom. I told him about my previous experience at church. I had observed that churches seemed to be all about themselves and that, while they talked a lot about outreach, they rarely reached out."

"And The Lighthouse is different from other churches?" asked Kevin.

"We have to be," Michael emphasized. "It's our third Beacon. I'll leave you alone so you can digest that idea."

For God is working in you, giving you the desire and the power to do what pleases Him.

Philippians 2:13 (NLT)

Do not withhold good from those to whom it is due, when it is in your power to act.

Proverbs 3:27

Beacon Number Three

Our church will be a beacon in our community.

Life is difficult. People in our community need love. They need hope. They need a place where they can find peace and comfort.

Our church will be a beacon in our community.

We will be a place of security and strength. We will be a place where people will feel safe from the pressures of the day. We will be a source of support in times of need and courage in times of challenge.

Our church will be a beacon in our community.

When a marriage is troubled, when jobs are lost, and whenever tragedy strikes, we will be a place of hope and prayer. We will be here to console and coach, to teach and support.

Our church will be a beacon in our community.

And how will this light shine? It will shine in our people and in the way we communicate and interact with each other and with those outside our church. We will share love the way Jesus did and teach the value of service the way He did. We will live a life of service. Every person has a role. Everyone has value. Everyone can serve. We are here to help and to love each other. Our example will be a magnet that attracts good while standing strong against evil.

Our church will be a beacon in our community.

The people of this area will know that they are always welcome here. This is the place where Love can be found. We will offer a smile, a hot cup of coffee, and a hug from a friend. We will offer sanctuary to those who need it.

We know it won't be easy. There will be those who will say we are motivated by members or money. They will watch for us to stumble and laugh when we fall. We will keep our eyes on our purpose and on the needs of our friends, neighbors, and strangers in our community. On the darkest days and nights, we will be a place of comfort and support.

Our church will be a beacon in our community.

A beacon shines during storms. It also shines when it is calm. Our church will be a place for celebration as well as crisis. It will be a place for conversation as well as comfort. It will be a magnet for the community. A place where friendships grow and new friends are welcomed. It will be connected to the community and will be a resource for anyone working to make our community better.

Our church will be a beacon in our community.

Kevin closed the book. "Michael, what does that look like – being a beacon?"

"The lights are always on. The door is always open," replied Michael. "And everyone in town knows it. Kevin, churches can be intimidating. If you are not a member, if you don't know someone, it can be hard to walk into a church, especially when it is not Sunday morning."

Kevin nodded. He had seen that kind of barrier before.

"Our building is used for daycare, town meetings, counseling, connections, you name it. We have a coffee counter and a free book exchange."

Kevin shook his head. "How? How do you find the time, the energy, the people?"

Michael let the question hang in the air a moment. Then he looked Kevin in the eye. "There's always time for what is important, Pastor. Being accessible, engaged, involved. This is what brings people to us."

Kevin was absorbing that thought. He was about to ask Michael a question when he noticed that the coffee shop was filled to overflowing. Every seat was taken and there was a friendly buzz in the air.

He looked around the room at the variety of people, and his gaze stopped when he came to Pastor Tom, who was deep in conversation with a young woman at a table in the back. He watched as the pastor prayed with her, she hugged him and she turned to go. As she left, an elderly man eased into her seat, shaking the pastor's hand. It appeared they were meeting for the first time.

"What's going on back there?" Kevin asked.

"Back where?" Michael turned. "Oh, I almost forgot. It's Tuesday. Pastor Tom has his 'office hours' here every Tuesday from 9am until."

"Until when?"

"Until there's no one else who wants to talk with him."

"These are church members?" Kevin asked.

"Sometimes, but usually not."

"So, random people just come in here to talk to the pastor?"

"That's pretty much it."

"Every Tuesday?"

"When we decided to be a beacon in the community, we started looking for better ways to connect with people who were not part of our church. Pastor started coming here on Tuesdays. Gradually, over months, word got around that there was someone here who could answer questions, offer advice and give counsel."

"We learned a lot about counseling in seminary but we never learned how to reach people like this." Kevin shook his head. "And all I had to do was get out of my office."

"Kevin, most of these folks don't have a church. They often don't even want a church, but they also don't know where to turn when they have problems. It's hard to reach those people sitting in a church office."

"It's also a great way to reach the unreached," said Kevin, halfway under his breath.

"Exactly," added Michael. "Turn the page. You are ready for Beacon Number Four."

But how can they call on Him to save them unless they believe in Him? And how can they believe in Him if they have never heard about Him? And how can they hear about Him unless someone tells them?

Romans 10:14 (NLT)

Beacon Number Four

We will reach the unreached.

Our job is to reach the unreached. The unreached do not know us and we do not know them. We must connect with them to reach them.

We will reach the unreached.

The unreached believe they don't need God because they don't know God. They don't know God because they have built walls in defense and ignorance. They think we will force our beliefs on them. They think we are weak and they don't want to be weak.

We will reach the unreached.

The unreached believe that God is only about the afterlife and the Church has no value in this life. They don't know the Peace and Hope that comes in this life through a relationship with Him. They believe church is a social club where people gather to meet and gossip. They think we are only for people who look and dress like us.

We will reach the unreached.

How will we reach these people? We will do as Jesus commanded. We will reach out to them. We will not wait for them to come to us. We will do as Jesus did. We will speak to them in terms they understand and we will use modern communication tools, just as He did.

We will reach the unreached.

What shall we say to the unreached? We will share our message of love, acceptance, and hope. We will teach that Christianity is freedom. That Grace is for everyone. We will teach that the Holy Spirit who comforts and guides us is within us all and is available through a relationship with Jesus. We will present our Church as a place of fulfillment and compassion. We will help people cope with the issues of today. We will help them understand the fulfillment to come with everlasting life.

We will reach the unreached.

Love, joy, peace, patience, kindness, faithfulness, goodness, gentleness, and self-control. These are the fruits of the Spirit and we will share them with everyone we reach. Our actions will demonstrate our compassion and concern, our openness and transparency. Everything we give away we will receive tenfold in return. When we share love, we will receive love. When we show kindness, kindness will be our reward. In demonstrating the fruits of the Spirit, the un-reached will come to know God in a new light. Over time, they will see in us a hope for them-selves, a hope they will want to share with the people they love.

We will reach the unreached.

And once we have reached these people, our connection will allow us to teach and share. Over time, our new friends will learn the truth about life. They will learn that God created us to have a relationship with Him that begins in this time, on this earth, and it never ends. They will learn that everlasting life begins today. C.S. Lewis said, "We aren't bodies that have souls. We are souls. We have a body." Our souls will live on, long after this earthly body is spent. We must work to reach the unreached souls of our community.

We will reach the unreached.

Kevin took a deep breath and closed the book. Michael was not alone now and he gestured to a man to his left.

"Pastor, this is William. He chairs our outreach com-mittee."

"Hi, William. Outreach? Right, I saw your billboard."

"Which one?" asked William. "We have several."

"So, you do a lot of advertising?"

"We don't think of it as advertising, Kevin, we ..."

"We talked about billboards, radio, social media – all of it – at my churches. Those conversations went nowhere."

"You decided you couldn't 'hype' the word of God, right?" William offered.

"I was taught that advertising, marketing in general, is envy, greed. It's 'Look at me. Be like me. Buy my goods.' We didn't want to 'commercialize' our church."

William laughed. "We heard those same arguments, Kevin."

"So what changed your minds?"

"We realized that it's foolish to think that advertising, by nature, is either good or evil. But, if it is bad – IF it is – isn't it the absence of God's Word that makes it that way? Isn't it the lack of love, compassion and peace? Wouldn't God's Word make advertising good?"

"I suppose." Kevin was thinking.

"In other words, aren't we the foolish ones to leave the most powerful forms of communication in the hands of the Devil? Aren't we supposed to share the Good News? Instead, we allow the enemy to control the air-waves and the magazines and the internet? Why should we make his job easier and ours harder?"

"So, it's not the medium?"

"It's the message, Kevin. It's the message." William studied Kevin for a moment. "We must deliver the message of Hope. We have to tell the people why we are here. They have to know where to turn when the time comes – when they need us."

"But shouldn't they already know?"

"Kevin, the unchurched have a very different view of what church is and what it isn't. If we don't tell them why we are here, we leave it to their own ideas or perceptions, or worse, to the messages of the enemy."

"So, you view billboards and social media and the like as … ?"

"Evangelism, Kevin." William let it sink in. "Whenever you share the Good News, it's evangelism, pure and simple."

"Simple," said Kevin. "That's a word that was seldom used in my churches. In fact, we seemed to work extra hard to make things complicated."

"A common problem, Pastor. We had it, too. Fortunately," William added, "we recognized the problem and promised never to go down that path again."

Kevin said goodbye to his new friends and left the coffee shop. His hands were shaking but not from the caffeine. He was shaking with excitement.

He rushed back to his motel room and spent the afternoon making notes and thinking of ways to apply the four Beacons at his next church. *His "next" church.* He realized that he now had a sense of hope for the future. "My next church," he said out loud. "Sounds good."

He slept well that night.

The Greatest Church in the World

Wednesday

Wednesday morning was cloudy and distinctly cooler than the day before, but Kevin didn't mind the chill. He was ready to tackle the next Beacon. His head was buzzing with ideas for his next church. He had received a text from Pastor Tom to meet him at the mall. He found him in the computer store.

"Churches are a lot like computers," Tom said matter of factly.

"How's that?" Kevin asked.

"Well, this company has twenty-seven different options for laptops. This other company has only three. The first company tries to be everything to everyone. It sells on price rather than quality. Buying from them is cheaper, but it is also complicated."

"The second company is focused on making their computers simple and reliable. They are focused on providing value. Their computers cost more but their customers are willing to pay more, which makes them more loyal." Tom paused.

"I don't think I understand."

"Would you rather be the church that offers everything to everyone or the church that is focused and simple?"

Before Kevin could answer, Tom continued. "Would you rather have 'customers' who are reliably dedicated or 'customers' who feel no commitment to your church?"

"That one's easy," said Kevin. "If complicated means commodity and simplicity means loyalty, I choose simple."

"Exactly," said Tom. "Our church was about to close because we had gotten too complicated. We were trying to be all things to all people. Our message was too confusing. We became a commodity in the church marketplace."

They had left the computer store and were headed toward the food court. "Here, let's take a seat while you read the next Beacon."

A Lamp on a Hill

For my yoke is easy, and my burden is light.

Matthew 11:30

Beacon Number Five

We will keep it simple.

Our job is simple. Our message is simple. Our purpose is simple. Our church struggles in complexity. We thrive in simplicity.

We will keep it simple.

When Jesus walked this earth, He spoke clearly and purposefully. His message was a message of love and hope, of grace and forgiveness. With parables, He took complex issues and made them easier to understand. In modern times, we have managed to complicate the message and compound the meaning. This has led to conflicting ideas and misunderstanding. People are confused about our purpose. They hear one thing and see another. They are conflicted because they see and hear conflict. From now on, we will simplify our programs and the result will be better communication, better understanding, and better results.

We will keep it simple.

A simple message, delivered simply, consistently and faithfully. While Jesus is the answer for every person, our church cannot be all things to all people. No church can. Thank God there are a lot of churches. Each church can find its own voice, its own passion and purpose, and its own audience. We will focus on our purpose and we will work to be dependable for the people who connect with us. We will be focused on God's vision for our community and the core values that guide our church.

We will keep it simple.

Complexity is confusing and unfocused. Complexity is like a thief in the night. It sneaks up on its victims quietly and without notice. Our church was once consumed with complexity. We didn't realize that our programs and processes overlapped. We didn't see that we were spending time without getting results. We were content that we were "too busy" to get everything done because there was so much to do. The cycle of busyness was frustrating and divisive. It drove away members and confused guests. We will not return to those days.

We will keep it simple.

Other churches might try the program of the day. They might even be successful with that approach. We will stay focused on our approach. Programs are not inherently bad, but programs that take away from our purpose are of no value. Any program or event to be considered will be evaluated through this lens of simplicity. If the program eliminates complexity and fulfills our purpose, it will be worth considering. If it replaces something else that was not productive, we will consider it. It's that simple.

We will keep it simple.

Kevin sat in silence for a couple of minutes. "Well," he said out loud. "I'll bet that was a tough one to get through the committee."

He thought about his churches and the church he had attended growing up. He could see now all the energy that was wasted, all the meetings that seemed just like the meeting the week before, all the talk without action. "Simple has to be better," Kevin said.

"Look around you at these restaurants," said Tom. "The ones with the longest lines are clearly defined. This one serves just salads. That one serves burgers. There's one that serves Chinese food. Simple is always better."

"But people like programs and projects," said Kevin. "Don't they?"

"Some do, but sometimes programs separate people rather than bring them together." Tom motioned toward the book. "Read number six. It's all about the people."

Let us think of ways to motivate one another to acts of love and good works. And let us not neglect our meeting together, as some people do, but encourage one another.

Hebrews 10:24-25 (NLT)

Beacon Number Six

Our church is our people.

Our building is our building. It is just a building. It is not our church. Our church is our people. It is a simple principle, taught through the ages, but it is so often forgotten and overlooked. We forgot that a building without people is not a church. We found that people, filled with the Word of God, are more than a building. They are the church.

Our church is our people.

We will invest in people. Only people yield a return. Our building will one day crumble and fall. It will be replaced by a parking lot or a shopping center or another church. Only people are worthy of eternal investment. People will age and they will die. But a person reached with the Good News is one more soul won for God and one more soldier in Heaven's army. That is an investment with eternal dividends.

Our church is our people.

Can a building make itself better? Can it multiply or duplicate itself? Can it testify to a stranger about the power of Jesus? No, it cannot. But a person can. One seed of the Gospel planted in one person can transform a helpless person into a person of Hope. And one person, armed with the Good News, can transform hundreds, thousands, literally millions of souls. People who invest in people reap a Heavenly return on their investment.

Our church is our people.

How will we invest in people? How will we keep our eyes focused on what matters most? Every day we will endeavor to touch, encourage, and support our people. Our people are ALL of the people in our community; those we call members and those we hope to help. Both are important. Both have needs. Both have much to gain and much to give.

Our church is our people.

The people who have heard the message and joined our congregation will make our church strong. We will nurture and support each other, and together, we will share the Word of God. Together, we will transform this community and that transformation will spread throughout our state and nation. We are but one small church, yet, just as one match can start a fire that can engulf a thousand acres, our light will burn bright within the eyes and hearts of our people, and wherever we go, the Message will go, too.

Our church is our people.

So that we may focus on our people, we will tear down the walls within our church. Our building has walls. These walls are necessary for support, privacy, and security. In a building, walls are important. They are essential to the structure. We have seen that people can build walls, too. When walls form around or between people, those walls can cause insecurity, confusion, and miscommunication. Walls that separate people are bad, so we will tear down the walls within our church.

Our church is our people.

Our church was once suffocating because of the walls between our people. These walls created doubt, vanity, pride, and exclusion. The walls that were meant to protect instead caused alienation and disenchantment. Our walls kept people out. They had signs that read "off limits," "not your job," and "mind your own business." Because of these walls, we lost dedicated people. And the people who wanted to join us found the walls too high to climb and too wide to go around. They felt unwelcome and they rarely returned after they visited.

Our church is our people.

How will we tear down the walls within our church? How will we break the silos, flatten the organization, and make our church more inclusive? We will put people first. We will encourage participation, new ideas, and new energy. We will invite differing opinions, for it is through new thinking that we will discover new opportunities for growth and positive change. New ideas will remind us of our guiding principles, our purpose. We will always filter every decision through those principles. Ideas that support those principles and advance the Kingdom will be incorporated, while those that don't will be discarded.

We will provide promise not programs, love not lectures, meaning not money, and care rather than charisma.

Our church is our people.

"Hi Kevin. I'm Keisha." Kevin tried to re-focus as he closed the book. Keisha took a seat at the table beside him and offered her hand. It was a firm handshake from a young woman in jogging clothes. "Sorry, I was out for a run when I got the call from Tom."

"Hi Keisha. I take it you're on the leadership team at The Lighthouse."

"You could say that. Technically, I'm the 'chairman' of the board, but I'm not crazy about the title."

"Chairman? But you're, you're … "

"Young? We focus on purpose and passion here. Seniority is a myth, anyway. We are all equal at The Lighthouse."

"What about institutional memory, history, tradition?" Kevin was searching for words.

"We honor our traditions, our history, and we value our senior members, Kevin. It is part of who we are, but it's not why we are here. Everything we do must be part of our purpose. We don't have time to do something just because we have always done it."

"Okay." Kevin looked at the book in his hands. "But what about the building? You can't ignore the building, can you?"

"Of course not. But that's another lesson for another day, tomorrow maybe." She smiled as Pastor Tom sat down with lunch for three.

They talked through lunch and into the afternoon as Keisha shared her story and her history with The Lighthouse.

"I met my husband at church," she said. "I know it's a cliche, but I think The Lighthouse saved us both. Now, we are part of something bigger than us. Bigger than we ever imagined."

"Keisha and I met at the coffee shop one day," offered Tom. "She was not having a good day."

"That's an understatement," Keisha interjected. "But there's nothing special about my story. Many people have come to know the peace and purpose I feel in the very same way. Beacons Five and Six are reminders that a church is only as strong as its people and it only grows or shrinks one person at a time."

"Well said, madam Chairman," winked Tom.

Thursday

Kevin had promised not to read ahead but it was all he could do to keep from reading the next Beacons. Instead, he re-read the Beacons he had previously discussed with the pastor and his new friends. They were starting to sink in and his notebook was filling up with ideas and thoughts. He jotted one last thought as he left the diner.

Abby wasn't at work this morning and he wondered why. He missed her smile. Keisha had asked to meet him at church this morning, so he hurried down the sidewalk. A car passed him with a window sticker that simply read **JOY Lives Here.**

"The Lighthouse, of course," he said out loud.

As he approached, he saw Keisha standing out front. She had traded jogging clothes for business attire. Black slacks with a matching jacket and a teal blouse. She could have been a bank executive or a college president. He wasn't sure.

"You didn't mention your occupation yesterday," he blurted.

"Oh, I'm a writer," she said nonchalantly. "Kevin, what do you see here?" gesturing toward the church.

Kevin looked around. It was just as he had seen when he arrived a few days earlier. "I see a nice, old church. Well-maintained. Clean. Happy. Oh, there's the car that passed me a bit ago. Is that yours?"

"What else do you see?"

"What do you mean?" Kevin asked.

"This is the next Beacon, Kevin. We have to stop and see our church the way someone sees it for the first time. Let's go inside."

A Lamp on a Hill

The Lord doesn't see things the way you see them. People judge by outward appearance, but the Lord looks at the heart.

1 Samuel 16:7b

Beacon Number Seven

We will see our church with visitors' eyes.

We know this church. We have seen it many times. We know every plant and tree. We know the color of the paint, the cost of the fixtures, and the day the new sign was erected many years ago. To us, our church is familiar, comfortable, and just as it should be.

We will see our church with visitors' eyes.

Because our church is familiar, we don't see the signs of age, decay and rust. We don't realize that the new sign is now 15 years old. When we look at our church, we see what a parent sees. We look with love, admiration, and understanding. We don't see what a visitor sees.

We will see our church with visitors' eyes.

When we come into our church, we see old friends. We know them by name. We know their children, their hobbies, their history. We have been with them through success and failure, through joy and loss. We are family and we have supported each other for many years.

When a visitor comes into our church, they see something different. They don't know us or our ways. They don't know our town and we don't know them. While we are greeting old friends, they are searching for a friendly face. While we are drinking hot coffee, they are thirsty for a smile. While we are distracted, they are distraught.

We will see our church with visitors' eyes.

Today, we will see our church as if for the first time. We will see the rust, the grass that needs to be mowed, the trees that need to be trimmed. We will see the confusion that comes naturally when one is new. We will make clear the entrance, the bathrooms, the children's area, the coffee shop – all the things we take for granted, we will see with fresh eyes and we will take nothing for granted.

We will see our church with visitors' eyes.

And since our church is our people, we will endeavor to greet every person as Jesus did. We will be glad they are here, whether it is their first visit or their fiftieth. Whether they look like "us" or not. If they have come to our church to worship, we will welcome them. We will speak to them, not as strangers or as friends, but as fellow human beings in search of the Peace, Love, and Joy that comes from a relationship with Jesus. Our eyes will say "I love you." Our words will say "We are glad to see you," and our hearts will rejoice that another soul has found its way through our doors.

We will see our church with visitors' eyes.

Keisha was sitting in the pew beside him as Kevin closed the book.

"Okay. I get it. The building makes a statement about the church, the people, right?"

Keisha smiled. "And the people make a statement about the church building."

"So how do you get everyone on the same page?"

"Practice. Purpose. Grace, when we fail. It took us a while to figure out who we were. We knew we wanted to be open to all people, but we also knew we couldn't be all things to all people."

"Most of the people that visited my churches never returned," Kevin lamented.

"Kevin, 8 out of 10 who visit The Lighthouse do return. And when they return, they join."

"That's amazing. How do you do it?"

"Most of our visitors have a pretty good idea of what to expect before they get here. They've heard enough about us, they are not surprised. Regardless, we work extra hard to make them feel welcome and comfortable."

"How do they know you before they get here?"

"It's all about communication and purpose, Pastor. Turn the page."

A Lamp on a Hill

If anyone speaks, they should do so as one who speaks the very words of God. If anyone serves, they should do so with the strength God provides, so that in all things God may be praised through Jesus Christ.

1 Peter 4:11

Beacon Number Eight

We will communicate better.

We have a story to tell and a message to deliver. The Good News cannot be shared without words, and words are pointless without understanding. Communication is key to our success.

We will communicate better.

First, we will communicate better within our church. We will never assume that just because we have always done something a certain way or called something by a certain name that everyone knows and understands. We won't fall into the habit of using church slang or unofficial code words when we share news, schedules or information. We will always communicate clearly, concisely and respectfully, so everyone, from the newest member to the eldest elder, will know of what we speak.

We will communicate better.

Those who have not graced our doors or heard the Good News are not our church – yet. They don't know us and we don't know them. They don't know what we stand for or what to expect when they reach out to us. With open doors, open hearts, and open communications, we will stay connected to our future members. We will be easy to reach, easy to understand, and quick to respond to questions or comments.

We will communicate better.

Communication is better when it is open, honest, and frequent. We will communicate seven days a week. While Sunday is the day designated to deliver the Message, Monday through Saturday are days when we can reinforce the Message and demonstrate the meaning of the lessons Jesus taught so many years ago. We will reach out to our church to remind them that every day is a day God has made and to remind them of their many blessings. We will remind them that there are no part-time disciples, we will communicate to them and support them through their challenges. No one complains when a spouse says "I love you" every day. No one will complain when we share and show love through our communication every day.

We will communicate better.

Our website will be a source of information and inspiration. It will answer the questions visitors and members most frequently ask. It will be up-to-date and fresh. It will be a source of encouragement to everyone who visits. And anyone who visits, young or old, new to our community or not, all will find a message that accurately reflects our church: our values, our purpose, and our commitment.

We will communicate better.

Our social media pages will demonstrate the personality of our church and the personalities of our church families. They will show the faces of our people, the events we sponsor and the resources we offer. We will use social media to give visitors a glimpse of our church so when they visit, they will feel more at ease, more comfortable, and will have a sense of who we are long before they cross our threshold.

Today, we will communicate better.

Jesus took his message to the people. He spoke to them in terms they could understand. We will work to communicate as Jesus did, through deeds as well as words. We will meet people where they are – physically, spiritually, and emotionally.

We will communicate better.

When Kevin looked up, he found the sanctuary empty. He stood up to stretch his legs. As he walked toward the altar, a door opened and Keisha emerged followed by a young couple. "Kevin, this is Abby and Nick. They are pretty new to The Lighthouse."

"I missed you this morning," Abby exclaimed.

Kevin stepped back. In her street clothes and with her hair down, she only vaguely resembled the young girl who had waited on him at the diner each day since his arrival.

"Abby! It's you!" She gave him a big hug. "Is that your car with the **JOY** window sticker?"

"How did you guess? Pastor, this is my husband, Nick."

"Abby has told me a lot about you, Pastor."

"All good I hope."

"Yes, sir."

"So, isn't this the greatest church in the world?" Abby asked.

"It does seem like it," Kevin paused. "Keisha said you are new here. What brought you to The Lighthouse?"

"I guess you could call it a crisis," Nick responded.

"You had a crisis in your former church?"

"No, it was a crisis in our marriage," answered Abby. "It was on the rocks and we were about to give up. We really didn't go to church before that. Didn't see the need." Abby grabbed Nick's hand and smiled. "Now, we're regulars."

Kevin turned to Keisha. "So, is marriage counseling part of your outreach?"

"No, we simply offer support, share God's message, and provide resources when we can."

Nick said, "We felt so comfortable on our first visit that we shared our problems and joined a small group that day. The people in our group really helped get us on the right track."

"We saw the Light in our new friends," Abby chimed in. "We wanted to know more. Bringing God into our marriage saved us, Pastor. Now, He is part of our home and our life and whenever someone asks why we smile, we give Him all the glory."

"So, you are disciples now?"

"We are followers and learners," said Nick. "Every day is an opportunity to understand more and an opportunity to share what we have learned."

"We spent a lot of time in seminary talking about making disciples, but when I brought it up at my churches, I was told to 'focus on our congregation.' We would 'work on discipleship later,' but 'later' never arrived. That was a mountain that was too difficult to climb." Kevin drifted back to the struggles he had experienced before.

Keisha interrupted his ruminations. "You've had enough for today, Pastor. Get some rest. Think about what you've learned. Two more Beacons tomorrow and then the work begins."

"Work begins? What … "

Abby gave him a goodbye hug. "See you in the morning, Pastor." She took Nick's hand and headed for the door. "Goodbye, Keisha. Thank you."

That afternoon Kevin took a walk in the park. The exhilaration of the previous days had been replaced with concern. He had hit a wall. The wall of discipleship. *Why was it so difficult at my churches and how does The Lighthouse make it look so easy?*

When he returned to the motel, he made lists of questions and challenges. Hours later, he fell asleep, pencil and pad in hand.

Friday

The week had flown by but the previous night was long and restless. Kevin was anxious to talk with Tom. To get some clarity. He was sipping his coffee when Abby came by.

"You look troubled, Pastor."

"I'm sorry, Abby. There's so much to learn and so little time. I'll be going home soon. I guess I'm a little apprehensive."

"Don't worry. God brought you here for a reason." Abby smiled her million-dollar smile. "He won't let you down."

"I wonder who my teacher will be today?"

"Don't worry," she repeated. "He won't let you down."

Kevin decided to drive around for a bit before heading to the church. He thought back to the experiences and lessons of the week. *What if I had taken the next exit or run out of gas sooner?* He saw another billboard. There was the Lighthouse symbol and one word – **LOVE**.

His phone rang, interrupting his thoughts. It was Grace.

"Is everything okay?"

"Of course," she said. "Great, in fact. I want to come see your town."

"My town? You mean 'this' town?"

"Yep. I'll be there about 5. Love you."

"Wait – ," She was gone and he knew there was no point in calling her back or trying to change her mind. She was on the way and that was that. "Cool." Kevin smiled. He put away the phone and headed to The Lighthouse.

Tom was waiting in his office. It was comfortable with big, soft chairs and it smelled of old books. There were a few photos scattered around, a couple of diplomas and certificates, but mostly the walls were filled with books. *Just right*, Kevin thought.

"Good morning, Pastor."

"Good morning, Kevin. Take a seat."

"I have some questions for you," Kevin began.

Tom interrupted. "Kevin, why do you think we are here?"

"Sir?"

"The church. What is our purpose?"

"To love God, to love one another, and to share the Good News. Right?" Kevin wondered where Tom was going with this.

"Exactly. And when we do that, what happens?"

"Well, we become disciples." Kevin paused as the lightbulb came on. "And, we make disciples."

"Disciples can be missionaries. They can also be school teachers or waitresses or business owners. They are moms and dads. Disciples are reflections of the love of Jesus. Beneficiaries of God's grace." Tom allowed those words to hang in the air before they started to sink in.

"So, being a disciple doesn't mean knocking on doors or handing out Bibles or traveling to far away places … " Kevin was thinking out loud.

"It can mean that," Tom said. "It can also mean living an ordinary life that allows the Spirit to shine. A life that attracts people who want the Peace, Love, and Joy that can only be found in Him."

Kevin was holding the book of Beacons. "That's it. That's the next beacon, isn't it?"

"I'll leave you alone while you read nine and ten. Take your time. I'll be in the sanctuary when you are ready." Tom left and closed the door.

Kevin opened his book to Beacon Number Nine.

For God, who said, "Let there be light in the darkness," has made this light shine in our hearts so we could know the glory of God that is seen in the face of Jesus Christ. We now have this light shining in our hearts.

2 Corinthians 4:6-7a

Beacon Number Nine

We will make disciples.

Every member of our church is gifted. Each has talents, strengths, and abilities. We will not hide our talents or assume they are not part of God's purpose. We will develop our gifts. We will share them with love. It is possible to give without loving but it is impossible to love without giving. When we love our neighbors as ourselves, we will share the love of Jesus and our neighbors will become our friends. Our friends will join our church, and the Light of our church will shine brighter.

We will make disciples.

Every member of our church has influence. Every member can make a difference in someone's life. A mother teaches her children. A business owner teaches his employees and customers. A welder, an engineer, a florist, and an artist. Each has a sphere of influence. Each can win souls for Christ. A preacher preaches the Gospel. Our members "live" the Gospel. When others observe how we live, they will see the fruits of the Spirit living in our church – our people – and they will come to drink from our well. They will come to learn more about the Man from Galilee.

We will make disciples.

And how will we act as disciples of our Lord? Some will take to the mission field in faraway lands. Many will tend to the mission field in our own backyard. We will share the Good News in our workplaces, the shopping malls, the schools, and hospitals.

Sometimes, when appropriate, we will use words. Always, we will use actions. We will show God in what we do and how we act. We will show charity where charity is needed. We will lend a hand where a hand is needed. When a brother or sister falls, we will help them up.

The people of our community will know this as a place of love and support where people are treated with dignity and respect. And a place where dignity and respect are expected in return.

We aren't perfect. We will occasionally stumble. We will sometimes fail. When it is clear our hearts are in the right place, when it is clear our intentions are pure, it will be clear we are working for a greater purpose. We will win the hearts and minds of those we serve, and they will join us as disciples of Christ, sharers of the Good News.

We will make disciples.

People are watching. They want to know what we know. They also want to know that it is real. They are watching to see if we walk our talk. We will work to be consistent even as our circumstances change.

When the sun shines, we will celebrate God's warmth. Likewise, we will welcome the refreshment and cleansing of the rain. When our economy booms, we will be thankful for the abundance. When work is scarce and jobs are few, we will be thankful for the opportunity to share and support. In all things and at all times, we will thank God.

We will make disciples.

Every Sunday and every other day of the week, we will remind ourselves of our purpose. We have been given a Great Commission and we can't keep it to ourselves or shun our responsibility. For it is only when we keep our purpose in the forefront of our minds that we will recognize opportunities to share when they present themselves. It is only then, when we will see the signs of despair or pain or loneliness, that we can know when to provide comfort and kindness. Every day presents a new opportunity to share the Good News. With open eyes, open hearts, and open minds, we will lean into those opportunities and we will build new relationships.

We will make disciples.

"Wow," Kevin said to no one. "Wow." He took a deep breath and turned the page to Beacon Number Ten.

You are the light of the world. A town built on a hill cannot be hidden.

Matthew 5:14

Beacon Number Ten

We will be a lamp on a hill.

Jesus told us we cannot put our light under a basket. We must put it on a stand where it can be seen and where it can help others. We will light our lamp and we will place it on a hill where it can light the way for many.

We will be a lamp on a hill.

Our lamp will burn brightly. Like a lighthouse, it will mark the shoals and illuminate the dangers. It will guide and direct. It will lead to safe harbor. It will brighten the night and stand guard during the day. Our lamp will act as a beacon of hope and a sign of encouragement.

We will be a lamp on a hill.

We possess a gift. A gift of Peace for today and Hope for tomorrow. It is the gift of understanding and Love. This Gift is ours to own. And it is ours to share. In truth, this Gift is most beneficial when we give it away. To give it away, we must meet new people, make new friends, and share the Good News with everyone we can. Our lamp will bring the lost to our door. And it will illuminate our path as we go to them.

We will be a lamp on a hill.

How will we shine? How will we share? How will we see the glory of God shine in the eyes of the lost? By example. By deed. By word. Each member of our church will add power to our lamp as voices add to a choir. We don't need to force our message on the lost. We need to live as Christ taught us. We will love God and love one another. We must pursue our purpose and work to be the best we can be. Carpenters will build. Teachers will teach. Leaders must lead. As we go about our purpose, we will share the love of God and it will shine in our eyes. People will ask "How do you find such peace and purpose?"

We will be a lamp on a hill.

Kevin closed the book. Then he opened it and read each Beacon again, one at a time. He made notes in the margins and highlighted certain words and phrases. Three hours later, he emerged from the office and found his way to the sanctuary, Pastor Tom stood silently near the altar. He smiled. Kevin held up the book.

"This breaks all the rules."

"Actually," corrected Tom, "it ignores the rules that keep churches from being successful. These are the guides that set us free. They are the reason we are still here."

"Clearly." Kevin was thumbing through the pages.

"So, do you still want to quit?"

"Quit? No. I just need to find a church."

"You've come a long way this week, son."

"That is an understatement."

"Any questions?"

"What was the turning point? When did you turn The Lighthouse around?"

"It was God, Kevin. The Lighthouse 'turned around' the moment we finally stopped wrestling and started listening." Tom leaned closer. "Church work isn't easy, Kevin. You know that. But, it is a lot easier when we do as we're told. These Beacons keep us on track."

"How did you … ? Surely there were disagreements. How did you overcome?"

"Of course there were disagreements. Once we adopted these guiding principles, those disagreements became fewer. Eventually, the people who wanted to fight came around."

"Surely, some left."

"Some did. But those who remained made us stronger. More purposeful."

"And how have you stayed 'on track'?" Kevin asked.

"We never lose sight of our purpose. Never. Before every meeting, before every event, we pray. Then we read one of the Beacons aloud."

"Really?"

"Really. It takes two minutes. Since every decision is made through the prism of these ten principles, it's a good investment of time."

"Every decision?"

"That's right. And anyone can stop any meeting to reference any Beacon at any time."

"Wow."

"We have a job to do, Kevin. We have to take it seriously."

"Of course."

Tom let that thought sink in. "The job is serious, Kevin. The work is joyful."

"Is it?"

"Every day, Kevin, we touch another life. Reach another soul for Christ. Every day is a new opportunity to grow in God."

"Every day ... " repeated Kevin. It was more of a question than a statement.

"Kevin. Look at me. Every day. Not just Sunday. Not just Christmas or Easter. Every single day. That's our job."

"How do you get it all done?"

"Our church is our people, Kevin."

"I know."

"I'm not sure you do," Tom lingered. "Those Beacons are not just for me or for our staff or leadership team."

"No?"

"Every member of our church has a copy, Kevin. Every member is involved in keeping us on track, spreading the Word, and sharing our purpose." Tom added, "The reason we are the church you see today is not just these principles. It is because these principles are known, understood and lived by every member of our congregation. It's as simple as that."

"Simple," Kevin repeated as if it was still sinking in.

Tom paused for a second. "Pastor, I met you last Saturday at 6pm."

"That's right."

"I would like to see you tomorrow evening at 6pm. Same pew as last week. I have a favor to ask."

"A favor?"

"Yes. I'll see you tomorrow."

An hour later, Grace pulled into the motel parking lot. Kevin hugged her. He kissed her. He looked into her eyes for what felt like five minutes. "I sure have missed you."

"Guess you need to aim better," she smiled. "Grab my bags. We have some catching up to do."

That evening, Kevin recounted the entire week, Beacon by Beacon, lesson by lesson. There was an endless stream of ideas, thoughts, questions, and "what-ifs."

Grace held up her hand. "Pause for a second. You don't have to tell me everything at one time. What do you think of the town?"

"It's great. The people are so giving and friendly. Not at all what I expected when I stumbled in here last week."

"I can't wait for the grand tour tomorrow," Grace said as she took his hand.

Saturday

The sun was out in full force Saturday. Kevin took Grace to the diner to meet Abby. They went downtown where she bought him a new tie at the men's store. He showed her the mall, the library, the park where he had spent many hours, and the coffee shop where Pastor Tom holds "office hours" on Tuesdays. The day flew by. As he dropped Grace off at the motel, he said, "I'll be back shortly. I promised the pastor I would meet him at 6."

"Take your time. I'll read this little book." Grace smiled as she held up the book of Beacons.

"How did you … Never mind. I'll be back soon."

It was just past dusk as he approached the church door. There was a warm glow inside and the door was unlocked. Just like last week.

Unlike last week, he felt optimistic and ready for the future. He took a seat and, like last week, he started to pray.

"God, thank you. Thank you for Grace, Pastor Tom, this church and the people of this community. Thank you." He paused and looked up. There were the now familiar eyes of Pastor Tom.

"What a difference a week makes."

"Yes, sir."

"Kevin, last week you called this 'The Greatest Church in the World'."

"It is an amazing church."

"I agree. It's not the biggest, or the richest, or the most perfect church, but it is great." Tom gestured toward the sanctuary. "This church is great because we are reaching souls for Christ."

"Clearly."

Tom picked up a copy of the Beacons. "With these Beacons, these principles we have adopted, any church can be The Greatest Church in the World."

"I see that."

"Good. Come with me." Tom motioned as he walked toward the hallway. At the end of the hall he took a seat on a bench. Kevin followed. "When you arrived last week, we had just held a church meeting."

"On a Saturday?"

"I guess you could call it a party."

"I'm sorry I missed it."

"You were just in time, Kevin. You see, last week I announced my retirement and the party was a celebration of the next chapter of our church."

"I had no idea. What do you … ?"

"I need to ask a favor, Kevin."

"Sure. Anything."

"Yesterday, you said you were ready to get back to work. You just needed to find a church."

"Yes."

"Well, you have found your church, Kevin. Tomorrow will be your first sermon at The Lighthouse."

"But … " Kevin was caught off guard. "But Pastor, I need to get back home – and I'm not prepared – I have to talk to Grace … "

Tom touched Kevin on the shoulder.

"Grace says it's okay. And she said you can handle it. I think she's right."

"Grace? You talked to Grace? Wait … "

Tom stood and opened the doors to the fellowship hall. Kevin saw tables and chairs. There was a buffet line. There was Janet, Nick, Abby, William and Keisha. He saw Michael and at least two dozen others. And he saw Grace, sipping a cup of tea and talking with a young couple. She turned and smiled as if it was perfectly normal for her to be three hundred and forty-seven miles from home in a strange town, a strange church, talking with strangers.

On the other hand, it really didn't seem that strange after all. It felt comfortable. It felt like home. There was a banner hanging on the wall. It read **Welcome, Pastor Kevin**.

Grace ran up and gave him a hug and a kiss. "Pastor Tom called me a couple of days ago and told me I should come."

"How did he know? How did he?"

"He never said. He just suggested it would be worth the drive."

Kevin hugged her and smiled. His eyes glowed. His smile turned to a laugh.

"What?" she asked.

"You were right.

"About what?"

"This town and this church are just what I need."

Sunday

The air was so clear Kevin could almost see tomorrow. He laughed at that thought. "Who can see tomorrow?" he said out loud.

The landscape was filled with color. Blue sky. A blanket of snow still partially covered the ground with bright green patches of grass shining through. There were half-melted snowmen guarding many of the front yards on the way to The Lighthouse. It was brisk, but it was comfortable, too. Kevin stopped at the diner for a cup of coffee and to review his notes.

He walked down Main Street toward The Lighthouse. He walked past the men's store, the bank, the pharmacy, and the funeral home. They felt familiar now. They felt like home. Tom was right. Things are always better in the morning. His first morning as Pastor of The Lighthouse.

The music came to an end. Tom offered the opening prayer. He said goodbye and stepped aside as Kevin approached the altar. There was Grace. A ray of sunshine beaming from the front row. He saw hundreds of faces he didn't know – that somehow he felt like he knew. They were all shining back at him. All waiting in anticipation. He could feel the Peace. He could feel the Love.

"Good morning. Welcome to The Lighthouse. I would like to share with you something I learned from second Corinthians, chapter four."

The beginning.

The Greatest Church in the World

Epilogue

The Greatest Church in the World is a real church in a real town with real people. It is not in every town, but it could be. The greatest church might be large or small. It might be in the heart of a city or out in the country. It could be in the U.S. or anywhere in the world. Being the greatest church is not a matter of size or income or ethnicity or economy.

A great church is a church that attracts people with Love and Hope and turns those people into Christ followers. Then it turns those followers into disciples. Those disciples live their faith every day and, by example, they attract other people who want to learn about what it is that gives such Peace, such Hope.

Great churches inspire faith and teach the lessons Jesus taught. Great churches reach out and connect with people. Your church can be The Greatest Church in the World. It can be a Beacon of hope – a Lamp on a Hill.

The city does not need the sun or the moon to shine on it,
for the glory of God gives it light, and the Lamb is its lamp.
Revelation 21:23

Be the light.

The Beacons

We will trust God.

Today, our church is new.

Our church will be a beacon in our community.

We will reach the unreached.

We will keep it simple.

Our church is our people.

We will see our church with visitors' eyes.

We will communicate better.

We will make disciples.

We will be a lamp on a hill.